The Call of the Wolves

The Call of the Wolves

Written by
Kelsey Thomas

This is a work of fiction. Names, characters,
businesses, places, events, locales, and
incidents are either the products of the
author's imagination or used in a fictitious
manner. Any resemblance to actual persons,
living or dead, or actual events is purely
coincidental.

Printed in the United States of America

First Printing, 2019

Author Photo Courtesy Ron Richardson

ISBN: 9781947656871

Butterfly Typeface Publishing
PO Box 56193
Little Rock, AR 72215

Dedication

This book is dedicated to my dad, the late William Thomas, whom I love and miss so much.

"Every great dream begins with a dreamer. Always remember you have within you the strength, the patience, and the passion to reach for the stars to change the world."
-Harriet Tubman

Table of Contents

A Note from the Publisher

Upon meeting Author Kelsey Thomas, I knew something was different. She was subdued, polite, and spoke with a quiet, yet assured confidence beyond her years. Instinctively, I knew that sitting before me was potential waiting to be realized. Her story, while fictionalized, is quite real. In my mind it represents the duality of life. There are times we are called to step outside of ourselves and be strong. I'm so proud to have had the opportunity to work with this young lady. Great things are definitely in her future!

Iris M. Williams

Acknowledgments

To my mother, Darlene Thomas, thank you for always being there for me.

To my family and friends, thank you for your prayers, love, and support.

To my fifth grade Literacy & Social Studies Teacher, Mrs. Caycie Fowler, of Downtown eStem Public Charter School, Little Rock, AR., thank you for helping me with my writing skills.

Introduction

One sunny day, as the grass blew gently in the wind, a girl named Kelsey sat below the sky. Above her, birds flew, and animals ran free around her. Kelsey noticed a gray wolf resting in the gentle breeze.

Why are you here? Kelsey wondered curiously.

The wolf settled his gaze on her briefly; then, he looked away.

Kelsey stood and walked slowly towards the wolf.

Instinctively, the wolf was frightened and attempted to run away. Before he could, Kelsey rubbed his coat softly and calmed him down. The wolf licked the girl's hand, and Kelsey chuckled as she realized the wolf wasn't dangerous at all.

Chapter One

The Sky Turns Black

She looked up and noticed that other wolves had gathered around her. For a moment, she was scared but quickly dismissed it as she knew that she was a girl of nature.

"I'm leaving to go find some berries to eat," Kelsey announced to the wolves.

To her surprise, the wolves began to whine and nudge her with their noses.

"OK," Kelsey relented. "You can come with me, but when nightfall comes, you'll have to return to your den because I can't take care of you in the dark." She knew they'd never be able to keep up with her.

After eating, Kelsey went into her den and rested.

Immediately, the wolves began to whine again. They saw something in the sky that Kelsey had not noticed.

"Stop whining," Kelsey commanded with annoyance. She thought they were bored and wanted to play.

Still, the wolves continued to whine until finally, Kelsey left her den to see what the matter was. The wolves lifted their heads towards the sky.

Curiously, Kelsey looked in the direction the wolves pointed to and noticed that the sky was turning black.

"That's odd," Kelsey said. "It is only 2 o'clock in the afternoon."

Suddenly, she understood what was happening.

Chapter Two

Something Mystical Happens

Kelsey knew what was going on, and that made her scared.

She quickly noticed that the wolves were guarding her, and she was impressed.

Then, she saw something that took her focus from the wolves. In the black sky, there was a portal, and something was walking out of it.

It wasn't human at all. It was an animal, an animal that looked like a wolf.

But black?

Kelsey had never seen a wolf like this one.

Its eyes were red with very large pupils. Its ears were big and pointy, and its tail was fluffy.

As the wolf flew out of the portal, there was a laugh, a huge laugh.

When the wolf landed on the ground, he looked all around like he was the king of everything.

Kelsey wanted to speak up, but something told her to keep quiet.

Once the strange wolf had its fill of gazing at Kelsey, he began to walk towards her. Kelsey was scared and started trembling as the wolf got closer.

His large pupils were as sharp as a cat's eye.

"Hello," the strange wolf said.

At first, Kelsey didn't know what to say or if she should say anything. However, she soon realized she had to say something.

"Hello," she said simply.

Kelsey's new friends growled at the strange wolf. Then, she heard another voice.

Was that the voice of a wolf, Kelsey wondered. *But wolves can't talk! Can they?*

But sure enough, the wolves began to talk.

This must be my imagination, Kelsey mused. *There is no way these wolves are talking!*

After some time, she accepted the fact that they were talking, and she began to pay attention to what they were saying.

"You can never rule the entire world," Kelsey interrupted the strange wolf.

With a big, evil smile, the strange wolf started to laugh.

"Hahahahaha, hahahahaha, hahahahahaha! You think that, but it is true. I can rule the world."

Then, something happened. Something mystical happened, something Kelsey had never seen in her entire life!

Chapter Three:

Leader of the Pack

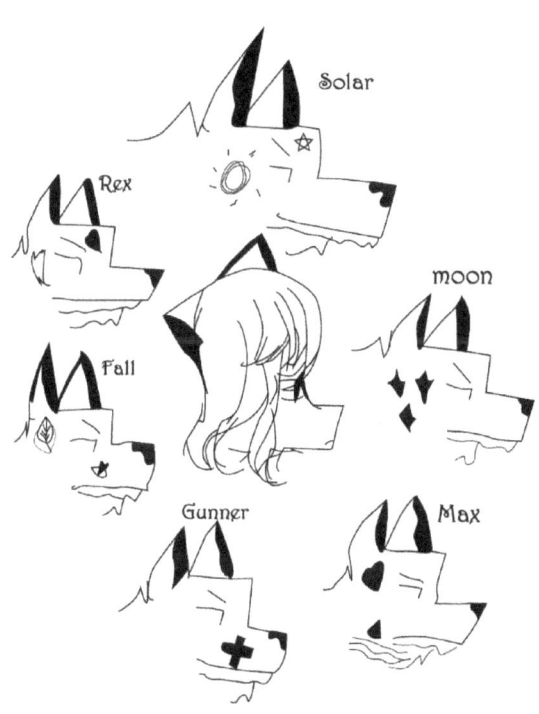

Each of the wolves that were protecting me turned into something I could never explain! Some wolves had striped patterns on their bodies; others had different shapes like stars, triangles, hearts, and even symbols. They were also in color as if they had dyed their fur!

Then, something happened to me!

I was turning into something too!

Suddenly, I looked like a queen, not the queen of nature but the queen of the wolves!

I couldn't believe it!

Was this *really* happening?

Yes, it was *really* happening!

The strange wolf was mad and frustrated! He knew he couldn't defeat a wolf queen, so he left.

"Goodbye," he said with defeat.

After he left, I turned back into my normal self, as did the other wolves.

Finally, I couldn't take it anymore. I had to know what was going on.

"What's going on?" I asked anxiously.

One of the wolves spoke.

"I am sorry for all of this chaos," he said with genuine regret. "But you see, this evil wolf named Krampus is out to destroy the world, and it is our job to stop him. The only way to do that is with your help.

I shook my head in disbelief. I understood him until he said they needed my help.

"My help," I said curiously. "What can I do?"

"You will save us," the wolf replied. "You are the queen of the wolves!"

This wasn't making any sense.

"How can I protect you?" I asked. "I'm only a human girl."

I was totally confused. I didn't understand what was going on.

Then, the wolf said, "I know that you don't understand, but I can help you to understand. By the way, my name is Solar. I am the leader of the pack."

Chapter Four:

Go! Now!

After hearing all of this, I knew I was about to go on a very important mission.

I had transformed into something I had never seen in my entire life, and that evil wolf, Krampus, was trying to rule the world.

This was serious!

But just to make sure, I decided to confirm with Solar.

"So, is this a mission?" I asked.

To my surprise, he simply replied, "Yes."

It was time for me to get to know the pack.

"What is your name," I asked the wolf to the right of Solar.

"My name is Moon," he said. "And to the right of Solar is Max. Behind Solar is Rex. He is actually Max's brother. The two wolves on either side of Rex are Gunner and Fall."

Once I learned the names of the wolves, it was time to get down to business.

"So, what do we do now?" I asked with determination.

Before Solar could respond, a flash of light appeared from the sky. A white wolf who looked like a female spoke. "Hello, my dear wolves! It is your queen's mother, and there is a mission I need you to complete!"

I stood there in complete shock. Then, the white wolf spoke to me.

"My dear daughter, I see you are noticing something that you do not understand. But don't worry, I will explain it all to you later."

I shook my head up and down and nodded in agreement.

"First," she said. "You will need some training to build up your strength so you can fight monsters and eventually destroy Krampus!"

Again, I nodded my head, but this time in bewilderment.

"Go to the kingdom," she instructed the wolves. "I must talk to my daughter!"

The wolves hesitated, so she shouted, "Go! Now!"

Chapter Five:

How Did I End Up Here?

Solar was the first to speak. "Yes, ma'am!" He said.

I watched in amazement as they used a portal to go to the kingdom.

When the wolves were gone and the portal had disappeared, the queen focused her attention on me. Her eyes were piercing.

Then, it was my time to speak. I had so many questions. "What is going on," I began. "And how am I your daughter!"

She immediately looked sad. "Look," the white wolf began. "I know you don't know what is going, so I guess

I'm going to have to make you understand by telling you a story."

I felt badly. I didn't want to frustrate her with my questions. So, I decided to sit still and listen.

"I'm sorry your majesty," I offered. "I don't want to frustrate you. I promise it won't happen again."

After hearing this, she looked happy, and there were tears in her eyes.

"Are you okay?" I asked, now concerned.

"Yes, I'm ok, and you don't have to call me your majesty," she said. "You can call me mom."

"Mom?"

"Yes, when you were little, you always called me *Your Majesty* whenever you would make a mistake," she said through tears.

"How did I end up here?" I asked.

Then, the white wolf, who said she was my mother, looked angry when she spoke. "It is all because of Krampus!"

"Krampus," I repeated. "How is that possible?"

Chapter Six:

Krampus's Motive

The white wolf took a deep breath and began her story:

"One night at your bedtime, when all the wolves were asleep, Krampus sneaked in your room and made you drink a potion that made you forget about us. He took you away to an open field and told you that you were a girl of nature. He also told you that it is your job to take care of all the innocent creatures here forever."

"What an awful thing to do," I cried. Then, I thought about something else. "So, wait a minute! Is this why we must defeat the monsters who are protecting Krampus' palace?

"Yes," the white wolf said. "Krampus is trying to destroy our kingdom, and he doesn't want you to remember who you are."

Now, I was angry too!

"Well," I said with determination. "I need to start training right away if I am to defeat Krampus! Let's go!"

But then, I stopped and turned around. "Wait! Instead of calling you mom, can I call you by your name? Is that okay?" I asked.

"Yes," the white wolf responded. "That is okay. My name is Star."

"Okay," I said with relief. "Thank you."

We stood there smiling at each other for a while; then, I began asking more questions.

"So, what do we do first?" I wondered.

"First, you must come with me to the kingdom," Star responded.

"Okay!" I agreed.

Star opened up the portal to the kingdom. I felt a very hot hand touching my shoulder as I walked into the portal. Then, I heard a very faint whisper. It sounded like Krampus.

"Give up!" The voice said. "There's no way that you can defeat me."

I stopped and looked back to see who was talking.

"What's wrong," Star asked.

"I thought I heard a strange whisper behind me," I told her. "But I don't see anyone behind me.

"Ok," Star said to me worriedly. "We'll talk about it later when we arrive in the kingdom."

I agreed, but I didn't respond. I didn't want Star to know I was afraid.

Chapter Seven:

Several Steps Backwards

As I entered into the portal, I felt a nervous chill travel down my spine. Inside the portal were so many different types of wolves. I couldn't count them all.

There were gray wolves, red fox wolves (wolves with fox fur), **arctic** wolves, and also black wolves. There were fury wolves and rare ones too!

Upon entering the kingdom, many of the wolves began to stare at me. Then, they came over to me in a hurry as if they recognized me and were excited to see me after so long.

It had been a long time!

Soon the word spread as they began telling other wolves to come over to where I was.

Then, I felt something!

It was something I had never felt in my entire life! I fell and faded into darkness.

It felt like no one would be able to save me.

Then, I heard screaming.

"Please," someone said. "Someone help her!"

Then, I saw a silhouette, a figure, a shadow. It was a wolf that I slowly began to remember. Instantly, I knew who it was.

It was Krampus – the wolf king of the demons.

There was a fog in the room that made it difficult for me to see him. Finally, the fog broke, and I was able to see him clearly.

He was very scary! His eyes were very dark, darker than the first time I had seen him. He looked a lot creepier than before too.

He was so menacing. I had to step back from him immediately.

"It's okay, child!" He hissed. "You don't need to be scared of me!"

Nonetheless, I already knew that he was lying. I took several steps backward.

I had a feeling that a fight was about to break out!

Chapter Eight:

Never Give Up!

I was so scared.

Is this a dream?

I wanted it to all be a dream, but I knew that it wasn't.

"Just come over here, child," Krampus sneered. "There is nothing to fear."

"No," I screamed.

"Hahahahaha!" Krampus chuckled and chuckled like there was nothing on his mind.

Then, in a split second, he leaped towards me, but I managed to duck and get away.

Now, I KNEW that this was a fight. It was time to get serious.

My body was still, yet it felt intense! I stared hard at my opponent and shouted, "So, you think you can get away with all that you've done?"

Krampus said, with ice in his voice, "Once you are dead, you won't be able to help your family or friends. You won't be able to help your mother either!" Then, he let out an evil laugh. "Hahahahahahaha!"

I felt like crying, but I knew it wouldn't help. I knew that a hero would never cry over negativity. I had to protect my kingdom.

Then, as quick as the light of lighting, Krampus pounced again.

This time, when I tried to get away, I felt a great pain in my neck which reminded me that I wasn't quick enough.

I fell to the ground with a hard *thump.*

"Do you give up?" Krampus asked.

I was about to give in until something inside of me reminded me that giving up was not the right thing to do.

I knew I could never give up.

"No!" I said with a renewed sense of fight. "No, I will never give up!"

Then, Krampus was gone.

I heard a beeping sound. My head was hurting badly, and I saw a lot of wolves around me. I had no idea who they were!

Finally, I heard someone say, "She's awake! She's awake! Kels is awake!"

Although my head cleared, I was still confused over what I was seeing.

"Who are you, wolves?" I asked. "And how do you know my name?"

I was frightened, but somehow, I
instinctively knew that there
 was nothing to be scared about.

"Don't you remember us?"

Chapter Nine:

Wolves with Power

I didn't know them.

"No," I responded. "Not at all."

Then, I heard the bang of a door being closed.

It was just what I suspected. A black wolf soldier entered the room and made an announcement.

"The queen," he began, "needs her daughter!"

I knew things were serious.

"Here I am," I responded. "I am the queen's daughter!"

"Come now," said the soldier. "This is very important!"

"Yes, sir!" I said with seriousness.

I got out of bed like a flash and ran quickly to the door. As we made our way out of the door, I saw a big kingdom.

It was bigger than all of the luxuries in the world combined!

The windows were huge, and the color of the kingdom was golden yellow. The kingdom glowed brighter than any star!

As I entered the kingdom, I noticed soldiers everywhere we turned. They looked very stern.

Ahead of me, I saw a wolf sitting on a throne. It looked like mom! I ran quickly towards her. As I did, a lot of wolves started to notice me. They were shocked that I was home.

I felt as though they wanted to hug me. Still, they knew that their job was to guard the kingdom which meant they had to behave appropriately. I felt their happiness anyway.

I stopped running and kneeled slowly to show respect for my mother.

"Mom," I cried. "I am here. Is there anything important you want to tell me?"

"Yes," she replied. "Come to me!"

Star and I walked into a room full of powerful wolves. I knew they were powerful and rare.

"Here," Star began, "is where you'll be prepared for the journey that you will soon begin."

"Cool!" I said. "So, what type of powers will I be getting?"

"You will not be getting your powers today," Star revealed. "You won't get them until tomorrow."

"Why," I asked, completely stunned.

Chapter Ten:

KELS!

Confusion was all over my face. I didn't understand why I couldn't get my powers now. Krampus had already nearly defeated me. I needed to be able to fight him now.

"Just not right now," Star responded with finality.

Although I didn't understand or agree, I knew better than to challenge Star. "Okay," I said.

"First," Star explained, "I will tell you what all of these powers mean."

I shook my head in agreement as I eagerly waited for her instruction.

"This one," Star said, "is a mystical but common, dragon spell, and this one is for wolves who go on various quests to defeat rare monsters, much like the one you probably saw outside! And this next one is a rare mystical half spell. They are a blend of bird, cat, and wolf."

I was transfixed as I listened to Star explain all of the powers to me.

"And this one over here is the rarest spell in all of wolf history. One of our ancestors had this, but no one knows who. All we know is that it is a secret."

You could hear a pin drop as a hush came over the room.

"The Gods of the wolves will pick a wolf from here when the time comes," Star explained. "This spell is a mystical ancient Greek spell. This means that every single type of wolf or wolf power combined creates the rarest wolf of them all. Only two wolves should have this power, but only one wolf, whom is one of our ancestors, has it. Again, no one knows who that wolf is. Do you have any questions," Star asked.

"No," I said quietly. "I don't have any questions."

"Good," Star said. "there's one more thing before we're done! You are also going to be able to stay here at the kingdom since you have come back."

"Really!" I said loudly. "That would be an honor mom!"

Star chuckled as she said, "Well then, I guess you should meet your brothers now since you're going to be staying with us."

"My what!" I said.

"Your brothers!" Star repeated. "Don't you remember them?"

"Not really," I confessed.

She smiled; then, I knew. It was the guards at the door. The knights I saw at the door were my brothers.

"Guards!" Star shouted. "Come! There is someone I want you to meet. Your sister has come home!"

"KELS," said one of the guards. "Do you remember us?"

"No," I said sadly.

"Maybe you'll remember us when we tell you our names," one of the guards said. "My name is Rex. We used to play all the time whenever I was on break."

I was trying to remember. Then, I did remember!

"I think ..." I began, but I was interrupted before I could finish my sentence.

A wolf came bashing through the door like she had lost her mind.

"YOUR MAJESTY! YOUR MAJESTY! YOUR ..."

And before she finished her sentence, she looked right at me and said, "IS THAT KELS?!"

Chapter Eleven:

The Five Shadows

Everyone was quiet.

"Uuuuuu!"

"Who are you?" I said.

Then, I remembered!
"Wait a second! Is that you,
Maddie!!"

"Yeah!" Maddie said. "You
remembered!"

Moments later, I fell. I fainted. All I
saw was darkness. I heard
screaming in the background. I was
scared. I didn't know what was
happening.

After several minutes of darkness, I
saw a shadow again. However, this
time, there were five shadows!

They looked like they did not play.
They looked serious, really serious.

Then, I heard laughing.

I was so scared. I didn't know what
to do. The shadows were wolves,
and the one in the middle began
walking towards me. He was coming
at a slow, but steady pace.

The more he walked towards me, the
more nervous I became.

I knew it was Krampus.

I was as still as a stone. I hadn't
known how powerful he was until
now, and I didn't like it.

I remembered the pain of him biting me on my neck. It was awful.

At a decent distance, he stopped.

My heart was pounding. His silence was making me very uncomfortable. So, to break the silence, I decided to speak.

Before I could utter a word, Krampus pounded his right paw to the ground quickly. It scared me so badly that I jumped.

My heart continued to pound really quickly. I still didn't know what to do.

Finally, Krampus spoke.

Chapter Twelve:

The Challenge

Krampus had a wide and evil grin on his face as he spoke. "We have come face to face yet again, haven't we?"

"Yes," I said as I did my best to look like I wasn't scared. "Yes, we have."

I don't think my bluff worked on Krampus.

Pretending not to be afraid only seemed to make matters worse as I did my best to be brave under the extreme stress.

Krampus was staring directly at me without blinking. The smirk on his face let me know he was a pro at this.

His gang were pros too.

Finally, I couldn't take it anymore. I lost my patience as anger took over.

"So," I said angrily. "What do you want, Krampus?" I was speaking as loudly as I could hoping that would prove I wasn't afraid of him or his gang.

Still, it didn't work at all.

I felt like a fool because Krampus and his gang weren't scared of me in the least.

Then, I saw the fire.

I had no idea what was happening until I saw a ton of wolves on each side. There seemed to be billions of them. Then, I realized what was going on.

Fire plus a stadium of wolves meant only one thing – a wolf fight! Again!

This time there was a huge difference. The difference was that this was not a one on one fight. Other wolves were watching. This could only mean one thing: I was going to be fighting in a stadium.

This was it. This was happening. Fighting wolves was going to be challenging, but I had to do it.

Chapter Thirteen:

Making My Struggle Worse

Krampus was chuckling. "Welcome to the arena of the demons!"

The audience was laughing and hollering.

I remembered the pain Krampus had inflicted on me, and I wasn't sure if I could do this. Nonetheless, I knew I had to try at least.

"You, my child," Krampus said, "will fight all five of us! If you win, I'll let you take a break from seeing me again! BUT, if I win, you'll quit saving the world, and you'll be my princess instead. Together, we will rule over the world!"

The thought of ruling with Krampus made me sick to my stomach. It also made me very angry.

"Together," I laughed. "That will NEVER happen."

"ARE YOU READY FOR THE CHALLENGE?" Krampus shouted. I think I hurt his feelings then.

I didn't know what to do. I didn't even think I was ready. But if I gave up, I knew I would never win. I had to do my best and try to do what was right.

So, I said, "Yes, I am ready for the challenge."

Krampus looked surprised.

I knew by the look his look on his face that he thought I was going to give up.

"Well then," Krampus said, "let the game begin."

The five wolves took their places. Four of them took their respective places in the corners of the arena. Krampus was in the center with me, three feet away from me.

I was terrified, but I kept my eyes on all of them as best I could.

All of a sudden, I heard a quiet voice.

I had no idea who it was, but I knew it was female. My mind was concentrating on what she was saying. I knew she would tell me what I needed to know to help me win this fight. However, before she did, the voice became silent.

Then, she left!

I was speechless! She didn't even tell me what I needed to know.

Suddenly, I felt really strong in my body, much stronger than I did before.

Did this quiet wolf make me stronger than before?

I didn't have time to find out because right away the battle began! In a quick motion, the wolf in the top left corner of the arena lunged after me. I jumped out the way in a second. He growled at me with furiousness in his throat and jumped at me again. This time, he jumped on top of my back and tried to bite me.

I was panicking now.

I was moving my body right to left and side to side. I wasn't thinking about anything but the wolf on my back.

Suddenly, another wolf came from behind me and tried to bite my leg.

I tried to be strong, but it was only making my struggle worse.

Chapter Fourteen:

Next Time

The fight was a struggle. I was outnumbered and struggling. I felt like I couldn't take it anymore! I wanted to give up.

Still, I had to do what was right! I couldn't let Krampus win!

Then, I burst like a flower. The wolves on my back let go and hit the ground hard. They were ferociously mad at me.

"Krampus! I thought you said that this girl was not strong!" One of the wolves said to Krampus. "Were you lying to us?"

"What!" Krampus responded. "No! This fight has just started! Keep fighting. She'll give up soon."

"I hope so!" The wolf said.

That's when I remembered these wolves. Way back, a long time ago, these same wolves were making trouble. They were Krampus's knights of the demon kingdom.

They were always trying to steal me from the kingdom. They knew that I had power and that I kept the wolf kingdom together. They didn't want that.

Now, I remembered who they were. The one who was talking to Krampus was named Alex! The second one was named Sylas! The third one was named Moth, and the fourth one was named Myth!

How could I have forgotten?

I called them by their names.

"What the -," Moth said. "So, you finally remember us now, huh! Maybe, you won't remember us when you die!"

Moth ran as fast as a cheetah and leaped into the air in slow-motion.

I should not dodge, I thought. *I have to make a powerful move! But what?*

I had no time left. I had to do something. Right when he was going to land on me, I jumped into the air too and pushed him to the ground.

He was frustrated. "I give up" Moth shouted.

"Why!" Krampus said.

"I can tell you're lying to us." Moth shouted again.

"I'm not lying," Krampus replied.

"I can't see anything, Krampus!" Moth insisted. "You have done enough! I'm tired of it! Bye!"

"What?" Krampus said, "This was the first battle you have challenged with Kels!"

"I don't care!" Moth replied.

I can tell Krampus was not happy with me at all. But I didn't care. I had defended myself, and I was happy that I did. I was very happy with myself.

"I'll get you next time!" Krampus vowed.

Nonetheless, I didn't really care. So, I said, "Hit or miss! I guess they never miss, huh?"

Krampus growled at me and tried to pounce on me, but I was able to get away. I leaped and scratched his face. He fell and looked weak.

I woke up and was now lying in bed.

Chapter Fifteen:

Goodnight World

My head was aching so painfully that I couldn't even lift it!

I wondered, *Why is it when I faint that I always end up fighting the demon wolves?* Maybe, in the future, I would understand.

"Kels! Are you okay? Please, say something! Anything!"

I wanted to speak, but my head was aching badly!

I tried to speak. "M-mom."

"Kels! I'll take you home so you can rest, okay," Mom said with concern.

"Ok," I said weakly. I felt sad about all that had happened. I felt sad for my mom. I know that a mother's job is to be a mom, and sometimes, that meant worrying for your children.

I was dizzy, and I found it hard to walk. By the time we made it to the kingdom, I couldn't walk anymore. Star had to carry me on her back. It was very embarrassing, but I just couldn't help it.

Once we got to the kingdom, a lot of the wolves, as well as the knights, noticed me. They quickly rushed towards my mom and began asking her a lot of questions.

I didn't really pay much attention to the questions they were asking. The excitement of the day had worn me out.

After my mom spoke to the wolves and answered their questions, she helped me to a new room that I hadn't seen before or at least that I could remember anyway.

My head was hurting so badly; I thought it was going to blow up!

Man! What was I thinking? Why would my head blow up?

I had to rest. So, Star laid me in the bed and left. The bed felt really comfortable and soft.

I could sleep for 48 hours straight, I thought.

But if I did, I would be in a coma, and I didn't want that at all!

Nope! No sir!

I finally fell asleep, and when I woke up, it was already nighttime!

Man, I thought. *I really needed that!*

I looked up at the sky and wondered what was in store for my future.

Would it consist of fighting monsters, going on quests, and eventually, defeating Krampus and his demons ultimately to save the world? That would be fun. Well, I hoped it would be.

I put those thoughts aside and focused on going back to sleep. I knew I was going to have a big day ahead of me.

I knew I'd have to be strong in order to face whatever would come my way.

Goodnight, world.

Chapter Sixteen:

Cutting in Line

It was 9:00 in the morning. I was still really drowsy, and my face felt really droopy.

The sun was shining brightly, like always, which was a good thing.

Best of all was the smell of beef jerky, lamb chops, and pork.

YUM!

Because of the smell, instead of being sleepy, I was now extremely hungry!

Licking my lips, I jumped out of bed and rushed quickly out of the room. As I ran out of the room, I saw a ton of wolves, but the only thing that held my attention was finding the source of the smell.

OH YEAH!

I quickly made my way down the stairs, rushed across the halls, and felt my stomach rumbling as I got closer to the food.

That's when I saw a long line of wolves in front of me.

Seriously! Are you kidding me right now! Do I really have to wait like everyone else? That's not fair at all!

I waited five minutes but soon decided that I couldn't wait any longer. I was going to cut the line!

That's right! I was going to cut in line! I was going to cut right in front of the first wolf in line! I didn't care if they were mad. I was too hungry to wait two hours in line.

There wouldn't be any food left!

I got out of line and made a mad dash for the front of the line.

"Hey," the wolf shouted angrily. "What do you think you're doing Kels?"

I didn't care that he was upset. So, I ignored him, which only made him angrier.

"Didn't you hear me," he yelled loud enough for the entire room to hear.

"Stop it," I said, wanting him to stop yelling at me.

Instead, he did something horrible. He pushed me and said, "That's what you get for ignoring me."

I fell to the ground hard.

Luckily, Star had witnessed the whole thing and had intervened before things turned into a total nightmare.

"Drake," Star said, "stop that now!"

"But Kels was the one who cut in front of me!" Drake protested loudly.

"Well, if she did, she did, ok?" Star said calmly.

"But-" Drake began to protest.

"No," Star interrupted him. "I've had a lot of issues already today Drake, and I don't want to deal with this today."

"But you don't understand," Drake persisted. "I was already in line. Then, Kels just randomly cut in front of me. I was just telling her it was wrong."

"Yes," Star said. "I saw that, but you yelled at her."

"I did," Drake agreed. "Because she made me angry."

"Drake," Star said firmly. "Like I said, I've had a rough morning, and

I won't deal with this too. So, please just stop."

"FINE!" Drake snapped.

Hearing Drake snap at my mother made me upset, and I wanted to hit him because he was very disrespectful to Star. However, I didn't because Star had asked us to cut it out.

Things settled down, and the crowd went back to what they were doing before the commotion.

Once I got my food, I stuck out my tongue at Drake and boy did that make him mad.

"Shut up," he yelled at me.

I winked at him and began enjoying what was absolutely the most delicious meal ever.

YUM!

Although Drake said things were fine, somehow, I knew that they weren't.

Chapter Seventeen:

Bewildered

As I was eating my food, Drake came over to me. I braced myself for an attack.

"You're a jerk," he said.

I didn't care what he thought of me. If he was having a bad day because of me, then that was his problem and not mine.

"No," I responded in the calmest voice I could muster. "Actually, *you* are the jerk."

"Oh yeah," Drake responded. "I can prove it to you."

"Show me," I pressed.

He did something that caught me completely off guard. He bit me on my right arm! It hurt badly and was bleeding hard.

I tried to remain calm but couldn't. Then, I screamed. All the wolves were frightened by my scream. Some probably thought I had to be dying because I was screaming so loudly.

I didn't care what they thought. The blood was pouring out of the wound and was running down my hand. I was shaking and didn't know what to do.

Drake just stood there and laughed hard.

That made me angry!

I was so mad. I punched him in his eye. Yep! That's right; I punched him hard.

He yelled from what seemed like his soul. His eye quickly turned purple. I had hit Drake so hard; I'd given him a black eye. He was furious now.

It happened again. I fell ill and realized I was going to faint! I saw blackness all around me. This time, I heard nothing. Then, I heard footsteps, loud footsteps.

The footsteps were coming right towards me. I got up quickly and tried to see who it was. Just like always, it was Krampus!

I was confused.

"Krampus," I began. "You said that-"

"Oh no, my name is Alfa."

"What," I said in bewilderment. "I thought your name was Krampus. I guess I made a mistake."

"Yep, you have!" Alfa said. "Anyway, I see that you have a large cut in your right arm. It looks DELICIOUS."

"Um, please don't say that Alfa," I said trembling. "That makes me uncomfortable."

"Oh," Alfa said. "I'm sorry. I didn't mean it like that! I'm just saying I am so excited to meet you!"

"Ok," I said, not knowing what to say. My heart was pounding.

The only thing I knew to do was to run, and that's just what I did.

Chapter Eighteen:

Dodging Traffic, Bullets, and Alfa

I ran as fast as I could! Then, right in front of me, I saw trees, cars, sidewalks, and humans!

What! But how!

Before, there was darkness! Now, there's a whole big world around me! I saw a stop signal ahead of me.

Should I go for it?

Well, a wolf is chasing me, trying to eat me alive, I thought. *Maybe I should risk getting hit by a car instead of being eaten alive.*

Soon, I realized that this wasn't the way a hero should think. I was a warrior, and I wasn't going to give up without a fight!

I remembered the Ninja Warriors that I sometimes watched on YouTube.

This is gonna be fun, I whispered to myself.

I was kind of scared but excited at the same time. Somehow, I knew that I could do it. Even though cars were coming in both directions, I believed in myself and knew that if I tried, I could do it!

I ran and suddenly (without knowing how), I began jumping over cars on my four legs, well, technically, not four legs. I meant my two legs and my two arms.

Since I am half wolf, I can say that, right?

I ran quickly down the sidewalk, made a sharp right turn. I almost fell. I bounced off walls and ran back into the street. I almost got run over, but I averted the car just in time.

Alfa was getting close now. I was out of breath, but I knew I had to keep going.

Some people were honking their horns and yelling at me to get out of the streets. Others said nothing. They were obviously shocked because I was running on four legs with a wolf was chasing me.

One person even tried to shoot us about five times, but missed. I don't think the person had bad aim. Alfa and I were just too fast. Alfa was dodging bullets, and I was dodging him AND bullets!

I was tired, and I could tell that Alfa was out of breath too, but he knew that we had to keep running and dodging traffic and bullets.

I darted around streetlights and mailboxes. However, there was more traffic. So, again, the only thing that I could do was run *on* cars. I literally had to jump from one car to another! I jumped on trucks too!

I was not really afraid of heights, but if I were on a tall building, I would for sure scream!

I knew what I had to do.

So, I thought, *let's hop to it!*

Chapter Nineteen:

A Plan for Alfa

I hopped on a taxi first; then, I hopped a Jeep. I could hear my feet clashing on the vehicles, and I'm sure the people inside the cars heard me too.

There were a lot of cars ahead of me, and I jumped over car after car and truck after truck. Finally, I began to get really tired, very quickly.

So, I began searching for somewhere to hide. I couldn't find a suitable place, and I couldn't run anymore. Just as I was about to stop, I found a place to hide – a dark alley.

After jumping down from the truck I was on, I ran quickly into the alley. I hoped Alfa didn't see me as I made my escape into the darkness.

Once inside the alley, I decided to hide behind a FedEx truck. That was when I saw a door. Instead of hiding behind the truck, I went into the door.

I had a bad feeling about that. The door creaked very loudly, but it was the only place I could find to hide from Alfa.

Quickly, I went through the door. For some reason, it smelled gross inside. The smell was old and rank like someone hadn't flushed the toilet well.

I knew what that smell was!

It was dogs!

They were cute, and there were so many of them I could hardly count them all.

Instantly, I made a plan, a big plan! I was going to give Alfa a BIG surprise - just for HIM!

In order for the plan to work, I would need to figure out how to get the key.

Then, I heard footsteps. I heard someone at the door. I heard a jingling sound and realized I needed to hide. The only place I could hide was behind the door.

It was Alfa. He had found me.

I sneezed because the air inside the truck was very mossy.

Alfa had found me!

He tried to get me and pounced quickly, but I was quicker. I slammed the door hard in his face and quickly locked the door.

Alfa banged and growled at the door, but he couldn't get in.

Thinking I was safe, I turned around, and there right in front of me, stood a man with the keys to the truck.

Chapter Twenty:

Just for Fun

I stood still, not making a sound, as did the man!

Then, Alfa burst his way inside the truck. He jumped on top of me. I was squirming and trying desperately to get him off. He was growling and trying to bite me.

During the struggle, I saw something glowing. It was Alfa's right paw.

I knew what it was. It was a type of spell that makes wolves evil. The only way to reverse the spell was to look them in the eye for ten seconds and say, "Don't be evil. Remember who you are!"

I wasn't sure I could do it. How was I going to get Alfa to look me in the eye for that long without trying to chomp on me?

"Get off of me, Alfa!" I said.

"No!" Alfa snapped.

While trying to get Alfa off me, the man, with the keys, just stood there staring at us. I'm sure he was confused and didn't know what to do.

To snap him out of his trance, I did the only thing that I could do – I bit him!

The man hollered. Then, he ran as quickly as he could through the door.

Alfa was continuing to lunge after me even after the man ran away.

I saw a portal appear ahead of me. I didn't care where it led! I wanted to get away from Alfa!

I ran towards the portal. Alfa was close behind me. I was tired, but I knew I couldn't stop running. I jumped into something that felt like slow motion; so did Alfa.

If Alfa had made it one inch more, he would have gotten my leg. In that instant, we were both inside the portal. There was darkness like before.

I tried to run away, but suddenly; Alfa scared me by jumping on top of me. He tried to bite my entire face off, or it felt like it anyway.

Just then, another wolf appeared in front of me, and of course, it was Krampus!

"Alfa," Krampus shouted. "You can stop now!"

"But master," Alfa said. "I am so hungry!"

"Grrrrrrrrrr!" Krampus growled.

"Yes, sir," Alfa obeyed.

"Krampus," I yelled. "Why are you doing this to me? I won, right?"

"Not really," Krampus said.

"What do you mean not really?" I questioned.

"You cheated," Krampus said.

"Cheated," I was confused. "I did not cheat."

"Whatever," Krampus said. "Anyway, I can't believe that you don't even remember Alfa."

"Huh?" I didn't know what he was talking about until...I began to remember something!

"Alfa," I said as I looked at someone I used to love. Then, I turned to Krampus. "Why would you do such a thing to him?"

"What?" Krampus smiled an evil smile and pretended to be ignorant. He said, "You don't want your boyfriend to be under my spell to be used for evil?"

"No!" I said. "Not at all! Krampus, please let him go be free!" I pleaded.

"No!" Krampus said with another evil grin. "In fact, Alfa, get her!" He commanded.

"No!" I screamed. "Krampus, what did I ever do to you to make you do these evil things?"

"Nothing," Krampus laughed. "It's just fun!"

"No," I sobbed. I was crying and begging on my knees for Krampus to stop.

There was nothing else I could do. I was helpless.

Chapter Twenty-One:

The Explosion

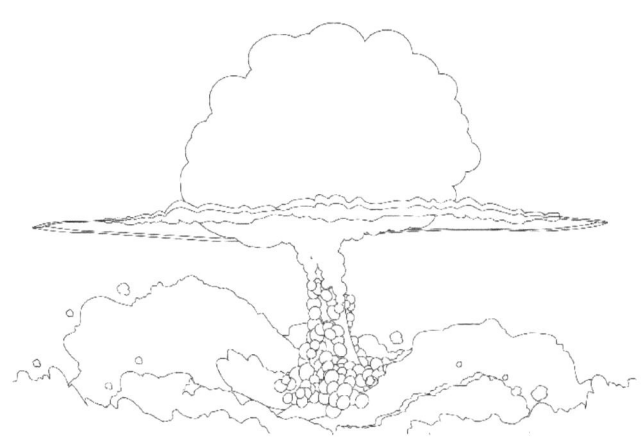

Then, Alfa did something amazing.

"No," Alfa refused.

"What!" Krampus said. "I thought you were hungry!"

"No," Alfa repeated.

I looked at him to make sure he was for real, and that's when I saw that the glow on his right paw was fading away.

But how was that possible?

I had no idea, but I didn't care. Alfa was changing back to who he really was.

"Alfa," I asked cautiously. "Is that you?"

"Of course, it is Kels," Alfa said.

Suddenly, Krampus was furious. "NO! NO! NO! NO! NO! NO! NO! NO!"

"Kels, we got to leave now!" Alfa said to me.

"But where?" I asked.

"Through here," Alfa said and pulled me through the portal.

I woke up in my room again. This time I saw Alfa lying beside me. I tried shaking him to wake him up.

When I realized it was night, I decided to let him sleep.

I laid my head on the pillow and snuggled up next to Alfa. I fell asleep too.

I didn't understand all that had gone on, but it was a lot. I was exhausted and knew I needed to sleep. I didn't know what tomorrow had in store for me, but if it were anything like today, I knew I definitely needed to sleep.

I woke up to the sun shining brightly. I heard something going on outside of my door. I got up to see, and as I opened the door, there as

Drake, the troublemaker doing horrible things as always.

I ran back to the bed to wake up Alfa. As he woke up, he hugged me hard.

"Kels, I am so glad that you are okay!"

"Same with you!" I said.

Then, we heard a loud boom.

"Uh, what was that?" I asked.

"I have no idea, but I think it's probably Krampus!" Alfa said.

However, it was an explosion that had hit the wolf kingdom.

It hit right next to where we were!

Chapter Twenty-Two:

He's Dangerous

F ire was everywhere. Rocks and glass were flying everywhere! Dust was getting into my eyes and throat! I was coughing so hard that I couldn't breathe!

It was the same for Alfa. He was hugging me hard, covering every part of my body as much as he possibly could, so the glass wouldn't fall on top of me.

We tried to get out of there as quickly as possible, but we were too weak.

I felt like I wanted to cry!

Was this the end of my life as a wolf warrior?

Immediately, I felt someone pulling me, trying to get me out of the dusty, smoky room! It was Star!

"Kel-," she stopped and became silent before finally speaking again. "Kels," she sounded angry. "WHO IS THIS?"

"It's Alfa!" I answered cheerfully. I thought maybe she was surprised that Alfa was here.

"WHY IS ALFA HERE, KELS?" Star asked furiously.

"Mom," I began. "Why are you so mad? It's just Alfa." I was confused.

"Okay, Kels," Star said. "I'll tell you later, but for right now, I'll have to get you two out of here."

Star tried to get me out first, and Alfa woke up. As he was trying to speak, Star yelled at him.

"Shut up," Star shouted as she began to cry.

Now, I wanted to know what was happening, and why was Star so mean to Alfa!

As Alfa was climbing out after me, Star scratched his left eye!

"Star," I yelled in shock. "STAR! WHAT IS WRONG WITH YOU?" I was furious now.

"Kels," Star said suddenly frightened. "All I can say is … HE'S DANGEROUS!"

"HOW?" I asked.

Then, I saw the lasers! They were destroying the whole kingdom!

"RUN KELS!" Star said.

Chapter Twenty-Three:

Protection at All Cost

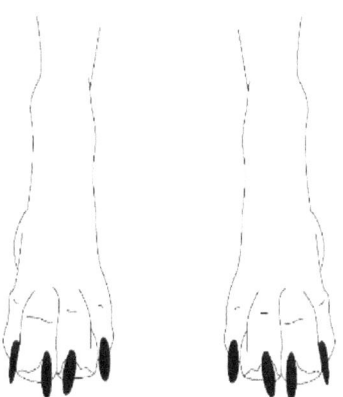

I was running, and Alfa was running with me. I didn't know where my mom was, but I couldn't look for her. There was chaos all around me.

Wolves were running all over the place! Some were even KILLED!

Then, I saw Rex. He looked more evil and scarier than before. When I saw him, he saw me. He was walking towards me. What I saw terrified me.

His eyes were blood-rose red and were absent of pupils. His fur was dark-devil black. His teeth were sharp as needles, and if touched by a finger, bleeding to death would be the result! Rex's nails were five inches long!

Then, Alfa stood between Krampus and me. Krampus looked mean.

"So, Alfa," Krampus said, "You don't want to work with me anymore, do you?"

"NO!" Alfa said immediately and without hesitation.

"Leave us alone!" I said.

Krampus was chuckling with glee. He continued walking towards us. I was hugging Alfa hard to keep me safe and warm. As I did, Alfa licked my face to remind me that he would protect me at all cost.

Alfa was as still as stone watching Krampus's every single move. I could tell he really wanted me to be safe.

I hugged Alfa tighter. He looked back at me, and that's when Krampus struck! He pounced on Alfa's neck and bit him. I screamed loudly and hard. I could tell Alfa was suffocating and getting weak. He was trying to be brave so that I wouldn't be afraid. Still, I knew he was in pain.

Then, with the little strength he had, Alfa bit Krampus's neck. Blood began spilling out from Krampus's neck as Alfa bit as hard as he possibly could.

I was so scared. Nevertheless, I knew I had to help. So, I bit Krampus's right leg. He whined and bit me back. I screamed in pain. I was terrified.

Alfa pushed Krampus away from me.

"Kels," Alfa said. "you're going to have to run."

"But I can't!" I said in pain.

Alfa lifted me as quickly as he could and threw me about ten feet away from the fighting. I still ran as quickly as I could in spite of the pain.

I looked behind me to check on Alfa. He and Krampus were still fighting. I wanted to stop to help Alfa, but I couldn't.

Chapter Twenty-Four:

Big Trouble

Krampus's gang was everywhere. They were killing as many wolves as possible. They were even killing the cubs.

I cried helplessly as I watched them get murdered.

All the crying and screaming was just too sad to watch, so I continued to limp away towards safety.

I saw one of the wolves looking at me. He looked similar to Krampus with a few slight differences. He smiled at me and began walking towards me. I started to run, but because of the pain, I couldn't go very far.

I yelled out for Alfa, but there he was lying in front of me, not moving.

But guess what?

Krampus was sitting right beside Alfa, smiling at me. Then, he and the other wolf started to run towards me. The two wolves grabbed me by the arms. I tried to get away, but their sharp teeth clung to my arms. It hurt really badly!

One of the wolves forced my head into something hard and nearly knocked me out. I was stronger than they thought. Still, they refused to give up and hit me a second time. This time, I blacked out.

When I woke up, I was in a big room that looked mossy and evil. The moss made me sneeze. As I wiped my nose, I continued to look around the room.

There was so much to see; it took a while for me to take it all in.

Once I was finished surveying the room, I thought about opening the door. I wasn't sure if that was a good idea or not. I didn't want to risk alerting the wolves before I had time to plan my next move.

However, I realized I had no choice. I had to do something while I could.

I decided to open the door.

Why should I be afraid to open a door?

Maybe it was the uncertainty of what was on the other side!

As I slowly opened the door, I saw a ton of wolves in a big group talking.

I was thankful the door didn't squeak or else I would be in big trouble!

Chapter Twenty-Five:

Braver Than I've Ever Been

As I watched them, more wolves came into the room. One of them looked like Alfa!

Good thing he's not dead, I thought.

"Here's Alfa's master," One of the wolves said.

"Good," Krampus said. "Take him into the room with Kels."

"Yes, master." The wolf responded.

They turned towards me and saw me!

I quickly closed the door a little too hard.

I shouldn't have done that, I thought to myself.

As the door opened, Alfa was dropped and kicked in his back.

"See ya later, you two!" One of the random wolves said.

"Whatever!" I said. "I don't have a care in the world about your discussion."

"Oh, you will soon enough," the random wolf said.

Then, we were left alone. I was so mad at them. *Why were they doing this?*

At least Alfa was alive and with me now.

"Alfa," I said tearfully. "Are you okay?

"Yeah, I'm okay," Alfa said weakly. "You don't have to worry about me."

"But Alfa," I said, feeling his pain. "You're hurt!

"Hey," he said. "I did it for you."

"I know, but…"

"But nothing," Alfa interrupted and put his right paw to my cheek.

I cried hard.

"Don't cry, Kels," Alfa said. "I'll be fine; I promise. I just need to rest. That's all."

"Okay," I said, shaking my head.

"At least I'm alive," Alfa said. "That's the most important part, right?"

"Yeah," I said, feeling hopeful.

"Well," Alfa said. "I'm gonna rest over there."

"Okay," I said as I watched Alfa get up and limp to the other side of the room.

While I watched him make his way to the bed, I started thinking that maybe he was right. At least he was alive, and that was all that mattered.

Alfa began having a bad dream while we both rested. He was making loud grunting noises and began failing all around.

I tried to ignore him, but ten minutes later, Alfa scared me when he woke up and yelled.

"Ahhh," I screamed too.

"Oh sorry, Kels," Alfa said. "I just had a bad dream."

"It's okay," I said. "What was it about anyway?"

"I don't think I want to talk about it," he said.

"Okay," I said, not wanting to push it.

As we were talking, one of the wolves entered the room.

"Hey you," he said looking at me. "Krampus wants to see you!"

"Who me?" I asked curiously.

"Yeah, you." He responded. "I'm looking right at you!"

"Hey," I said, now angry again. "You don't have to be rude, you know!"

"Just be quiet," he said rudely. "And come with me."

"NO," I said in a voice that was braver than I ever remembered.

Twenty-Six:

A Gruesome Sight

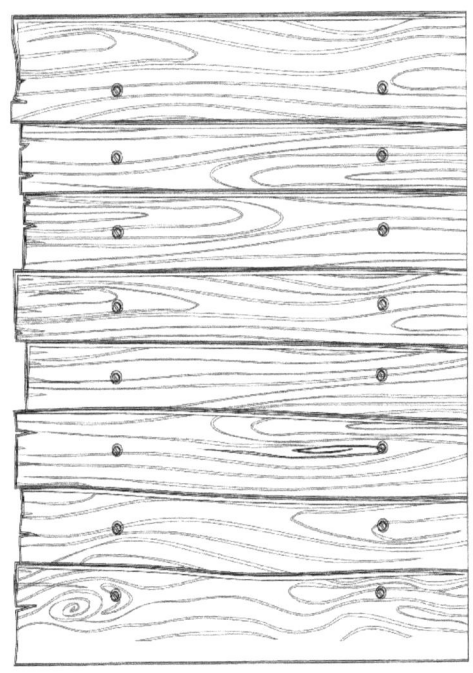

Although I sounded brave, I was more afraid than I'd ever been. I did not know what he was going to do or say.

"So," he said. "You think you're brave huh?"

I was so scared I could hardly breathe. I took a step back from him.

"Oh," he sneered. "You're not so brave after all, and your luck has run out!"

"What are you doing?" I asked, nervously.

His eyes were now as red as Krampus's.

He leaped towards me!

Alfa noticed and pushed me out of the way, right before the other wolf pounced on me.

Instead of pouncing on me, the wolf pounced on Alfa! Without a second thought, Alfa bit the random wolf hard enough to reach the bone of his neck.

It was a gruesome sight!

I held my neck and realized that Alfa had just saved my life!

Conclusion

Krampus slammed through the metal door and furiously hit the wall. Alfa and I jumped. Krampus' gang surrounded us. I wanted to run and was scared to face them. Alfa looked like he was thinking the same thing. We both were worried and scared.

I looked down and saw a big rock and a long stick. I had an idea! A GREAT idea!

I would run as fast as I could, grab the stick and throw it into one of the windows behind them. Then I'd throw the rock at Krampus, which would give Alfa and me time to jump out of the broken window and make a run for it.

This was a risky idea, and I knew anything could wrong. But it was more dangerous for Alpha and me to stay here.

Sizing up the window, I decided that the possibility of death was great, but I HAD to do it. There wasn't any other choice.

While Krampus continued to talk, I grabbed the stick and threw it has hard as I could. Glass flew everywhere with most of it falling on his gang.

They whined, and I knew I'd made them angry.

Quickly I grabbed the rock and aimed it directly at Krampus' eye. It hit him, and it seemed my plan was going well.

Alfa and I jumped through the window and landed hard, but to my surprise, we didn't get hurt.

We landed on our feet and began to run through the woods.

We were free and happy.

Suddenly I heard a voice. It sounded familiar.

Had I heard it before when I'd gone through the portal with Star as we went to the Wolf Kingdom? Whose voice was that?

About the Author

Kelsey Nicole Thomas was born in Little Rock, Arkansas on November 29, 2007 to William and Darlene Thomas. At the age of three Kelsey began reading and as she grew older her favorite story to read was "The Story of Ruby Bridges" whom she finally met in person at the age of eight.

Growing up in a Christian-based home, Kelsey confessed her life in Christ and was baptized at the age of five. At the age of eight, her dad who was her best friend passed away suddenly. Although this was a very difficult time for her, she continued witnessing to others about her belief which helped her through the tough times.

Kelsey is a member of Second Baptist Church on John Barrow Road in Little Rock, AR. where her Children's pastor is Pastor Jarvis Carrigan and her Senior Pastor is Dr. Kevin A. Kelly. She is an active member of the Sunday school and the Children's choir.

Kelsey also plays the piano and was a student for four years at R &C Hillman School of Music where her piano instructor was Minister Robby Hillman.

Kelsey composed her first piano music piece which was recorded and played at her dad's funeral service.

Kelsey enjoys playing with her two-year-old male Havachon named Pepper, Anime and Manga drawing, singing, dancing, and writing.

Kelsey is a student at Downtown eStem Public Charter School where she has maintained the honor roll from kindergarten years at Williams Magnet Elementary to present.

Kelsey's family is very proud and supportive of the young author and look forward to even more publications and accomplishments.

Butterfly Typeface Publishing

"We Make Good Great"

Contact us for all your

publishing & writing needs!

Iris M. Williams

PO Box 56193

Little Rock AR 72215

www.butterflytypeface.com

www.ingramcontent.com/pod-product-compliance
Lightning Source LLC
Chambersburg PA
CBHW072124170626
46813CB00004B/1684